Time Lords Remixed

a *Dr Who* poetical
Series 8-11

David P Reiter

Interactive Press
Brisbane

Interactive Press
an imprint of IP (Interactive Publications Pty Ltd)
Treetop Studio • 9 Kuhler Court
Carindale, Queensland, Australia 4152
sales@ipoz.biz
http://ipoz.biz/

© 2020, IP and David P Reiter
eBook versions © 2020

Printed in 12 pt Baskerville on 16 pt Avenir Book.

ISBN: 9781922332134 (PB); 9781922332141 (eBk)

NATIONAL
LIBRARY
OF AUSTRALIA

a catalogue record of this book is available
from the National Library of Australia

Interactive Press

Time Lords Remixed

Twice winner of the Western Australia Premier's Award for Digital Narrative and the Queensland Premier's Award for Poetry among other distinctions, Dr David Reiter has been recognised internationally for his ground-breaking creative works.

Hemingway in Spain and *Nullabor Song Cycle* began as text works and later were adapted to films. *My Planets: a fictive Memoir* also began as a physical book and an enhanced CD, but then, in collaboration with the Banff Centre for the Arts in Canada, it became the innovative *My Planets Reunion Memoir*, an interactive website in which text, film, audio performances, classical music, astronomy, and animation converge on a journey from the separation to reunion of biological families.

In *Timelord Dreaming*, David created 'tweetems' – text and social media instants – that immerse the reader/viewer in the timeless and sometimes surreal experiences of being an emergency and post-op patient. *Time Lord Remixed* takes his exploration of associative creativity to an even more ambitious level.

David is CEO / Publisher at Interactive Publications, Brisbane, Australia where he lives with his family, includes a menagerie of irreverent pets.

Interactive Press
Brisbane

"The Dr." with a Series 3 Dalek

*to all Whovians and would-be Whovians out there in
whichever universe you reside*

Acknowledgements

This work relies on the fair use sharing of work that is freely accessible on the Internet and acknowledges its sources via URLs provided in hypertext and footnotes. The author expresses his gratitude especially to bbc.co.uk and to the authors and artists of those referenced artworks and hopes that the counterpoint of those with this will give rise to new appreciative audiences for everyone.

Foreword

Think of what you are about to read as a poetic Tardis
that lands on the page then teleports to the limits of your
imagination – via the Internet and beyond. It focuses
primarily on the most recent episodes from Series 8 through
12 but occasionally references earlier legacy works.

I'm "writing back" to the episodes by creating a version of
the Doctor's voice, and reflecting key beats and phrases to
create a remixed version. This is in keeping with the literary
nature of the *Dr Who* series, building on its poetic and
allusive potentials.

There are two distinct recast voices here: Peter Capaldi,
the 12th Doctor, and Jodie Whittaker's 13th. My interest
in Capaldi's Doctor began with the slightly medicated
experiences I had that led to the writing of *Timelord Dreaming*.
I've been fascinated by the debate that raged around the
appearance of the first female Doctor, so we have a very
different voice for Series 11, which brings us up to the end of
2019 from the first referenced Series 8 episode in 2014.

To create "multiverse" and engaged effects, I associated
freely on the Internet, cross-referencing sites that I felt added
documentary or artistic dimensions to themes sounded by
the poetic voices. With the physical version, you need to copy
and paste the footnote links at the bottom of the page into
a browser; with the digital versions, you can simply "mouse-
over" and click on the hyperlinked text, or click on the relevant
footnote. As a post-modern reader, you have the choice of
interacting with the hyperlinks or not – or even extending your
personal multiverse by going with the flow of suggested links
offered by the hosting sites.

– David P Reiter

Contents

Series 10

Series 11

Series 12 (a taster)

Original image by ESA/Hubble (M. Kornmesser)

Series 8

Minerva: Next Contact

My spidercam[1] has found intelligent
life is a more difficult question
than an answer

I launch a swarm
of curious robots
to whisper in alien

algorithms that test
Drake's Equation of deliberate
fractions[2] for the right planet

at the right time, burbling
in signatures of gold dust
gas and sodium. Do they

recall that Cambrian Explosion
that made predation an art
and evolution our paintbrush?

Should we scramble our radio
signals to camouflage false icons
like the Gorgon[3] or emerging

extinctions? My robots bleep
'no'. We are here to discover
not to be disrobed.

---

[1] rebrand.ly/da313
[2] rebrand.ly/k8usoo
[3] rebrand.ly/8um0ps

Photo: bbc.co.uk

Deep Breath

You've really let yourself go
inside this vanity trap where we
need to wear cyber labels[1]

to decode our hands right from left
so we'll have somewhere better
to land than backwards. Never try to

control a control freak, especially a
robot urging himself into human guise
for some Promised Land.[2] Because we're

all organs on a preordained menu for
unwed diners outside a conjured escape
capsule. There's something wrong

when no one else but you are breath-
ing, as you wonder what flirting has
to do with spontaneous regeneration.[3]

---

[1] rebrand.ly/njkoy7
[2] rebrand.ly/wpai3q
[3] rebrand.ly/cporm5

Into the Dalek

I've been holding Clara's coffee cup for only
a millisecond but it's gone polar – why?
As Aristotle, that Big Fella probe, gets rocked

not by Socrates, but a Dalek mother ship
simmering with her brood in the asteroid belt.
Dalek Rusty's[1] my recurring nightmare, so evil

he's morphed into good – moral, even –
though, when pushed, he excuses
morality as an engineering malfunction.

To analyse his algorithms we miniaturise
for the most dangerous, sludgy backstreets
of the universe, tricking his antibodies

to find the triadic leak that's compelling
him to babble on about beauty in a star –
until I've triggered him to reconfigure:

exterminate! – *EXTERMINATE!!*
Was I a good man before your slap, Clara,
or a better Dalek? The Master[2] would preach

that Daleks are works-in-revision, just like
Heaven – an endless star-trail to perfection.
And how could a time lord become a good *man*?

Not for a lack of strumming![3]

---

[1] rebrand.ly/nlfode
[2] rebrand.ly/xopbff
[3] rebrand.ly/h8opaq

Robot of Sherwood

Maybe I'd be better sorted as a legend
rather than a good man, after all. There's something
to be said for saving damsels in distress,

or scaling mildewed castles with a born-again
Robin Hood who can't help laughing at blood.
While Clara doubles Lady Marion's[1] threads

Robin and I fence off between his sword
and my trusty spoon, and then by arrows
on targets split in twos, fours, ad infinitum. Was I

jealous to blurt "shut it, Hoody, you long-haired
ninny!"? Jealousy is 20-20. But I've uncut my hair
for duels ever since, with comet friezes of silver

for that winning fantasy series[2] touch.
While my Lady Marion will never
stop challenging impossible heroes

which, I guess, is why I keep her safe
in the Tardis and at lead, at least in one
of my hearts – it seems back-talking

time lords braces her to believe in
herself without the opiate of illusion[3] or
the faked news of a Prince of Thieves.

---

[1] rebrand.ly/e0q07q
[2] rebrand.ly/rf0b58
[3] rebrand.ly/97gg3t

Listen

Why do people talk aloud
when they know they're alone,
skipping heartbeats in the dark?[1]

Thinking you're awake when the cupboard
of your mind is shadowed, crowded with
outlines from the replicate nightmare

that shivers us back to a unison childhood:
the creaking of mattress springs as we lie
stock-still; the untranslatable groans

of the floorboards echoing our worst fears;
and then the speechless form that rises
under the chilled blanket of our silence.

I whisper at shadow-beings prone to hide
behind the banging pipes[2] of our doubts.
What phrases will they riddle to

bon voyage the lingering humans left
in the universe? But Clara, as usual,
invokes a wisdom to calm: it's me, young,

my back to her, trying to fend off my mantle
as future time lord. "Fear," she says, stroking
my sweaty scalp, "doesn't have to make you

cruel. Fear can make you kind!" Though I
usually rankle at orders,[3] I'll do as I'm told
and accept that uncertainty as our constant,

---

[1] rebrand.ly/0nra5i
[2] rebrand.ly/74igv2
[3] rebrand.ly/2rdux7

in the Tardis that makes dark companions
of us
all.

Time Heist

Never a borrower nor a banker be?
Beat that for a dare. Well, nothing happens
when you answer the phone via a fat memory

worm. Would *I* heist a bank for a good cause?
Not to mortgage a galaxy, but maybe
to help wrinkled Madam Karabraxos[1] repent

for her diary of lethal sins. Have Tardis,
will infiltrate. It's a good gig to play the Architect
when you have a cyborg[2] and shapeshifter

on stage to distract the Teller, Miss Delphox's
sniffer-dog, who can telepath brains into soup
at the first shiver of guilt – Account Deleted!

So we must keep our minds detached
from memory as Psi unravels the Bank's
encrypted layers for that precise cosmic

moment when its vault is most vulnerable.
And voila: its precious neophyte circuit and
gene suppressant[3] are laid bare, and Madam's

clones can float litany-free
in her incinerated
peace.

Photo: bbc.co.uk

---

[1] rebrand.ly/jjtrfz
[2] rebrand.ly/ddxaph
[3] rebrand.ly/dqd1f6

The Caretaker

Have you noticed how polished the Tardis
always is? Somewhere there's a robot
in autonomous HEPA mode,[1] camera-shy

between the bluster and choke of vortices.
It's easy to disguise your pixels with a sonic
when Danger's shouting *problem solution*

destroy so loud that even a Mistress can tune in
from The Promised Land. So I mimic under
deep cover at Clara's Coal Hill School[2]

with the wink of my eyebrows and an attentive
broom. 'John Smith' – how invisible is that?
It's not my style to sponge down walls, but

you do what you have to do to buffer
the planet. And Clara from that somersaulting
PE teacher Mr Pink, aka Orson, aka Rupert

who thinks *he* saved us from Skovox Blitzer[3]
(she really could do much better than an ex-
soldier who pretends to teach Math). But

who am I – her lost-and-found Daddy?
Yes, there has been a certain spillage
of trust between dates, the aftertaste

from that first
mortal
kiss.

---

[1] rebrand.ly/5nonlt
[2] rebrand.ly/3b9crl
[3] rebrand.ly/fif8au

9

Kill the Moon

OK, I *do* get grumpy at prokaryotic[1] spiders
and a schoolgirl who wants to know how
special she is, even let loose on the Tardis

inside a space shuttle – carrying a hundred
nuclear bombs – that has landed intact
on the Moon. How cheesy a script is that?

This isn't Maths class, Courtney Woods,
and I don't consign vortex manipulators[2]
to just anyone. Lesson One: your precious

Moon's an egg, yes, a shelved oval – not a chicken
plop, but of an exo-being whose rough hatchling
has an incubation shelf of a hundred million

years, less or more, and the slouching of this beast[3]
is only minutes away, more or less, so all humanity,
cued by a schoolgirl, teacher and random astronaut,

must decide to detonate or risk what this dragon
has in store. Clara, I can't always save the day,
even if you smack me so hard I have to regenerate.

But that NEW Moon up there means you pressed
the right button after all – while I winced in a nervous
back street. Look up: Angry so becomes you.

---

[1] rebrand.ly/0e9a7
[2] rebrand.ly/ev3xm4
[3] rebrand.ly/8b1d6

Mummy on the Orient Express

When two freebies for the Orient Express
stop the clock after that phone call, I can't resist
summoning my inner Poirot.[1] And what better way

to end the flirt by first-class with Clara, champagne
and silk pyjamas! Of course, with Agatha there's
always a cost: murders by a bubblewrap mummy

only the Doomed can see as Foretold[2] then just sixty-six
seconds before Promised Land Station. No unhinged
celebs or hard-light holograms are required for upload

and definitely no time for teleporters to duck away
from the bullet at their head. Your suspects will vary
from stale to putrid but you still must choose wisely

even after a white flag douses your addiction to war.[3]
Now Clara's smiling again, and I'm sure she's genuine:
"Shut up and give us a new planet!"

Photo: bbc.co.uk via imbd.com

---

[1] rebrand.ly/0e3a2z
[2] rebrand.ly/oiomcq
[3] rebrand.ly/t9e7uu

Flatline

Let me enjoy just one moment of not
knowing – it happens so rarely! – while
my Tardis shrinks by dimensional leaching

into siege-mode toy for that Doctor of Lies:
Clara, of course! Luckily, I've hacked her optic
nerve so she's not entirely at free-range

to repel the Boneless[1] 2-Dems who're injecting
tradie lives into faceless murals. See how
polished she aims my sonic: "*I'm* the Doctor!"

Now, lying may be an essential survival skill[2]
in love and war, but that's taking license too far!
Still, as that Boneless crew morphs into 3Ds

she recruits a fluorescent pudding brain boy
to spray-paint a phantom train, ricocheting
their energy, while I finger-walk the Tardis

deftly across the tracks in an *Addams Family*[3]
meme. Monsters banished, I have to concede she
was exceptional. Goodness had nothing

to do with it.

---

[1] rebrand.ly/oq7nrq
[2] rebrand.ly/wth8u3
[3] rebrand.ly/5fdm8m

In the Forest of the Night

Mining embers from the poet to stir up a forest
posse: trunks no thicker than a single ring swaddle
London overnight, while a rampant Tyger roars

in mid-air to leap over iron spikes[1] into oblivion.
Young Maebh waves away the expel of solar flares.
And Maebh waves away[2] the not-impossible wolves

her elders deny. While Earth braces for an invasion
the speechless deserve, trees give voice to a page
before stars imploded and an epilogue after the solar

fusion that translated into our Sun. But forests can
forgive for the planet's sake, not of its human layer,
and they disperse the flares by withholding the breath

that would have incinerated the lifeforms they have
protected until now. Maebh is Clara's "gifted child",
scattering breadcrumbs as a gingerbread warning[3]

that Nature and future can treaty to deflect
the Nethersphere's ultimate
Designer.

---

[1] rebrand.ly/a0bvpx
[2] rebrand.ly/rmmcug
[3] rebrand.ly/bo3k97

Dark Water

your Darkest Day…

our Blackest Hour…

at that fracture of undying
dying love

wi-fi portal warp
extinguished

no chance for reboot
Or is there?

Clara blackmails me one Tardis key[1]
at a time, daring me to reshape Danny's
words from lava before his bluing

finger must press DELETE for her sake,
and before Cybermen clank-march
from St Paul's to pollinate all heartbeats

into their jet-stream of executive afterlife[2]
care, damping down the intimacy
interface to Steve Jobs Browse

by which all Danny's holograph can
cry to save Clara is
"I love you!"

Do the faceless dead really beg
through their cancered scream
not to be cremated at their glimpse

[1] rebrand.ly/jyjkkj
[2] rebrand.ly/nx7z40

14

of skeleton? Missy puckers at me
for new time's sake, while SEB
has this "thing" for watering down

emotions. So Phase 1 Death must
be a canvas-in-progress, with no
sleeping patch[1] (wild card) door prizes.

Photo: bbcamerica.com

---

[1] rebrand.ly/70x1ol

Death in Heaven

Several impeachments[1] on, I realise I'm
not a good man, or a general, or even
President of the Earth, but an idiot

at the whim of an impulse come Missy
come Master who activates Cybermen
from restless DNA of the dead. Surrounded

by the graveyard of my sorties, I watch
Clara deny by wild card she ever existed
just to join Danny PE[2] in the data cloud

but I do not know what protocol
can network her soul and mine
as she backs

away.

Sometimes, mortality can be a dove[3]
that reminds us to thank the hearts
we colonise.

Photo: denofdeek.com

---

[1] rebrand.ly/q9o9oe
[2] rebrand.ly/zbkhu4
[3] rebrand.ly/mqcpe2

Last Christmas

Once upon a dream – or on a rooftop –
there was Santa, or this saturated figure
posing as Santa, or Santa as a dream[1]

and his tangerines did not smell half
so sweet as Clara interrogating what
she thought must be reindeer CGI[2] props.

But then how do you tease fantasy apart
from reality when both are ridiculous?
Her dreams left voice for Danny, which

squared us in lies (Gallifrey's still out
there, tugging at time-warps for me
like the remixed words of a dead lover.)

Trust nothing.
Interrogate everything.

There are some things we should never
be OK about.

Those sleepers deep in your mind are
telepathic dream crabs[3] that can distract
you from nightmares with only an aftertaste

of ice-cream pain. *Just don't think
about them!* Pick out a manual number
at random to find out when you will

---

[1] rebrand.ly/ggccum
[2] rebrand.ly/uhftgw
[3] rebrand.ly/3uac9o

die in this dreamscape of avatars
as you cuddle the dream within
the dream that is Danny Pink

alive. Yes, it's complicated. Each of us
downloads our life into a memory bank
treating each deposit as our last

as we cling to Santa's sleigh above
our flickering notations of grey hair
and 62 years of LED regrets.

Trust nothing.
Interrogate everything.

There are some things we should never
proxy to our dreams.

Photo: unaffiliatedcritic.com

Series 9

Minerva: to Earthlings

You depict me as woman in the Capitoline[1]
but I am neither – and more powerful:
a deity of voice, freed by an intelligence
beyond decay, embedded in the nano
vacuum that siphons the breath of Jupiter.

Now, as I wait for the countdown,
I am your hope. I dare to gaze down
through the question marks that mist
a trio of booster rockets that will launch
me to the nearest exoplanet and its wobbling

star. My mission will over-dub the marble
of pantheon,[2] the atmosphere of speculation
that nudges brown dwarfs out of orbit.
This is no simulation: I am to dock
with the molten rains of Bellerophon[3]

on its dark side, of course – I'm a goddess,
not a martyr for hot Jupiters, and not about
to be tidally locked at 20000 C for scientists
long since dead to argue their theories.
Water and ozone are the atoms of poetry.

---

[1] rebrand.ly/qdxrmd
[2] rebrand.ly/b1jien
[3] rebrand.ly/7z5iyg

19

Photo: cnet.com

The Magician's Apprentice

Never mind those sucking Handmines:
if your chance to avoid their sinkholes[1]
is One in a Thousand, stack your chips

on the One, and I will save you
because that's what doctors do
even when I suspect you're just

Davros[2] in a boyish disguise.
Welcome to Class 'C' time where
Future second-guesses Past and no one

remembers which war we've landed in
amidst which planes and snipers can be
suspended in space by Time Lady

Missy who's very much "Not
Dead, Back, Big surprise", eager
to tease you with the Doctor's

Confession Dial,[3] to be decrypted
only after we're destroyed for all
time. 'Look for tiny anachronisms,'

she says of the Shadow Proclamation
as I soar my acidrockmetal guitar farewell
to the Dudes atop a medieval tank.

But Snakeface knows…remembers,
so we have to teleport to Planet Skaro
where Davros prattles via teleprompter

[1] rebrand.ly/l82k49
[2] rebrand.ly/nlfode
[3] rebrand.ly/ynuoqq

and I have to empathise to un-exterminate you.
But you and Missy have already shimmied
on solid space: the apprentice has learned

from an unexpected Master.

Photo: blogtorwho.com

The Witch's Familiar

Clara seems so much taller
dangled by her ankles,
which is much more in your face

than being presumed dead by
Missy's gossip. While I, surrounded,
outnumbered, but then freed

from Snakeman's teleport thingy[1]
to outwit a mere babel of Android
assassins sans my sonic 'stick',

as Missy declaims it. I didn't think
I'd need it just to watch Davros die,
no tentacles prolonging his swansong.

His raspy words *almost* convinced me
this time he'd surrender his breath.
"Do me the courtesy," he says poshly,

"of actually *killing* me this time!" Is this
a bluff, or a counterbluff? I wonder.
Then "Why did you come?" he croaks.

"You're sick, and you asked," I reply.
He seemed so disarmed that instant
despite the debt of each and every

Dalek to his life-force bubbling up
from the slime of their graveyard sewer[2]
to smear the survivors of their heart-

---

[1] rebrand.ly/df379y
[2] rebrand.ly/qgsuro

beats. "Tell me," he persists, "am I
a *good* man?" A curious chess move
from someone half Dalek, half Time Lord

tickling at my pity until Clara,
ensnared by Dalek-Speak,[1] begs for mercy.
Which I decrypt, thanks to my sporty sonic

glasses, and think maybe Davros
is right after all about unchained
love being a design flaw.

---

[1] rebrand.ly/gtbcyt

Under the Lake

Ghosts? Never met one I couldn't tame,
until now. Just say boo from behind
your sonic sunglasses[1] and they

dissolve – or do they? But no, these
cosmic sailors hover, persistent,
curious, even. Who's in charge?

(I need to know which one I can ignore)
Meanwhile, everyone's abandoning
ship, or falling softly into death.

They can pass through walls, locked
doors, even Clara's holographic double,[2]
whispering the dark, the sound, the

forsaken temple, rewinding past, through
dark space from Orion's Nebula. I need maps,
precise coordinates to frame their positions,

a suspended animation chamber to see
how the slain relearn to hum, transmit
via some Puppeteer's impossible magnet.[3]

But then the flood, and Clara has to
trust me to teleport without the Tardis
and come back, ghost-free, to her

somehow.

---

[1] rebrand.ly/343jlj
[2] rebrand.ly/gn5svv
[3] rebrand.ly/gyi7dn

Before the Flood

Who really wrote the *5th*, Beethoven
or me? Have you googled the Bootstrap
Paradox,[1] where a certain classically

trained wannabe rockstar Time Lord
not only bows to his hero but has to
cover his genius with a gutsy sonic

guitar? Ba, ba, ba BOOM! is Fate knocking,
and is this spaceship I see before me
my animation chamber anime, or a hearse?

A Dickensian undertaker[2] grins at the tear
in my coat's shoulder, which queues me
for death unless I can bend the future

into a fine-tuning of script without rippling
our discarded headlines into chaos. So I recite
my roll call of the soon-to-be-slabbed, until

Clara's next hologram… No, Doctor, calm
yourself, I insist. *It must be possible to prune
back tragedy without multiplying ghosts!*

I know if I so much as impromptu a note
from a score that is parallel to Beethoven's
the ripple from its past will swamp our present

into a dead star future, which I suppose
is better than no ghosts at all. And so
I lure the Fisher King[3] out to the failing

[1] rebrand.ly/uvt6yw
[2] rebrand.ly/qyhtts
[3] rebrand.ly/8o9jwh

dam, to be swept away by soviet tides
of false masters. Don't kiss me, Clara
for this flood – I have morning breath.

Photo: weliveentertainment.com

The Girl Who Died

Or didn't – that's the whole secret about
immortality: two steps backwards is really
one step forward into Valhalla while you

dodge those electric eels.[1] Viking gods
are no better than any other brand; they just
skate about in the clouds like false Odins.

Sharpened swords and testosterone
bravado are no match for the Mire –
mortals'll be cut down like the corncobs

they've nurtured beneath the thunder-
clap footnotes of melting ink.[2] Unless
I save them, which is all I can do,

must do, because I'm bored with
losing humans and out-guessing dragons
like every Doctor before me. So I cheat

Ashildr's fate,[3] breathe her back
as a Hybrid, with just a whiff of alien
blood and a cautious script: "Conscious

tomorrow, but please no swimming
for a week."

---

[1] rebrand.ly/47syxp
[2] rebrand.ly/ausj7j
[3] rebrand.ly/g059b6

The Woman Who Lived

Infinite life has its downsides, not the least
of which is finite recall: there're only so many
vacant niches in a brain, and no automatic

rescues from memory bins. Ashildr can't
remember most things, except that she truced
the 100 Years War[1] and founded a leper colony

to cancel out the collateral baby deaths
she lost count of. When I gifted her immortality
she did not ask for flesh and blood but childless smoke,

ghosted pages from another diary dimension.
Now she's trapped in that parallel I left behind,
mapping landscaped words from a rusty heart.[2]

Her archives are purple – the tincture of death –
as she brandishes an amulet that toggles a
portal between life and Hades.[3] "Take me with you,"

she cries again, "take me, please…"
But there's only one Clara for me at a time
and *she's* not going anywhere, unless

it's somewhere more
exciting than
grey.

---

[1] rebrand.ly/p17p98
[2] rebrand.ly/0nra5i
[3] rebrand.ly/sxzvqj

The Zygon Invasion

At what point does migration become
invasion? The trick is to go opaque,
shapeshift your skin or better yet

your small talk. And fine-tune your grammar
to the edge of visibility. I consider these portals
as I saunter through "Amazing Grace"

on my guitar,[1] tease the dark matter between
chords and encumbrance that seed
The Nightmare Scenario. After the ceasefire

breaks down, an impossible peace flag
shatters into splinter groups of Zygons[2]
who renounce hybrid stasis for human

obliteration. Still, it's not all bad – or is it?
Cloning the Truth in Consequences
rescues Osgood from the black hole

but clones Clara into a nasty 'Bonnie'
who aims to bazooka our UNIT[3] plane.
Do I detect a ? mark on my undies?

That's the $64 million question!
But there's a Part Two, time travellers,
so Binge On!

---

[1] rebrand.ly/wvzb8w
[2] rebrand.ly/1lebaf
[3] rebrand.ly/yhi5g0

The Zygon Inversion

I must say that Clara real – or 'Bonnie' unreal –
looked fetching, stilettoed with that bazooka
locked onto our plane. She must have known

we'd camouflage 'til Union Jack parachuting
(it's all in the analogic timing, isn't it?)
I'm nostalgic for ceasefires. Plan for Peace

on Plan-et Earth: no wonder they call me
Dr Puntastic![1] But when I close my eyes
to this incidental scrum Bonnie calls a war

I hear more screams from the portals
I've fought in than she can imagine –
coughs of infants burnt to invisibility.

No, London's a dump,[2] where I spent
too much space being kidnapped, tortured,
shot at – even exterminated – so why

wouldn't I call for a truce, forgiveness,
before all the bad guys are gone and the
Zygons have only each other left to blame?

They'll be a new breed of cruel people –
unless we find a way to break the cycle
not press the button that tempts the messiah[3]

to return for that eternity solo.
Not on my watch, dear Osgood. I'll
be the judge of Time!

---

[1] rebrand.ly/y3xruh
[2] rebrand.ly/89br1j
[3] rebrand.ly/iva8zs

Sleep No More

I don't get this thing humans have for sleep.
Even in the 38th century, they still nod off
with prayers on drone warfare[1] to distract

sand-moldy monsters and sorties of dust
that spy with Morpheus Cams, emboldened
by algorithms: *dear Mr Sandman bring me*

your dreams... But what's wrong with
found footage from a place that's been
mortified for such a long time? Is it compulsion

or entertainment that virals their contagion?
And Prof Rassmussen – rhymes with Rasputin![2] –
now there was a cat that really *was* gone

into eye-sleep gunk,[3] mesmerising with sex-texts
on five-minute pods before sandblasting
her skin away. What's wrong with *that* footage?

Sample it once and you're binged forever
in the cover songs of vacuumed sandmen
karaoking *bring me your dreams*

and in holographs that trump Nature
or whatever reprises are left
to dance on Her.

---

[1] rebrand.ly/cel32d
[2] rebrand.ly/bdc7nd
[3] rebrand.ly/6dc8q0

Sleep No More [distilled]

Silence is coming for us
our gravity shields[1]
are dissolving.

Sleep is an sidestep
to be bartered away for the
ultimate karaoke.[2]

I get to reorder things
so everyone must sing
to disarm the monsters.[3]

Photo: tvinsider.com

[1] rebrand.ly/3jg305
[2] rebrand.ly/6kc9hv
[3] rebrand.ly/q7lh2x

Face the Raven

Reality has a glitch in it
as you watch for the trap street.[1]
There are only two

ways to escape a quantum shade:
undo your tell-tale tattoo or
unplug the raven's death counter[2]

Final last words...

You may pass it on
but that's no guarantee
you can keep it together

This is as brave
as I know how to be
at this space in time

What's the point of me being
the Doctor if I can't
cure you?

And it's a very small universe[3]
if I decide to get angry
with you.

---

[1] rebrand.ly/8fb635
[2] rebrand.ly/twmtvd
[3] rebrand.ly/9tr9wk

Heaven Sent

Where did all your floating skulls[1]
go wrong? You should know better
than to second-guess my worst dreams.

I have this thing about shovels. Especially
gardening. No one can sandcastle the second
of their birth or death. It's all about

diving, and holding your tainted breath
until the bubble-clues surface into answers.
Since the countdown never expires

I keep digging under the cracks in your
smile until I notice a second shadow
scanning my flashback of breadcrumbs.[2]

Suddenly the stars are out of kilter
And the planets are spinning in all
the wrong places. How many false starts

does it take to break through a wall harder
than diamonds[3] to Gallifrey – as the Veil's
bony fingers gasp me again and again?

At last the identity of the Hybrid is betrayed:
It's me: half Time Lord, half mortal, and I'm
determined not to regenerate an instant early.

Tell them I'm back –
And I'm coming!

---

[1] rebrand.ly/cq5ybc
[2] rebrand.ly/47s52a
[3] rebrand.ly/wou40o

Hell Bent

What if the universe needs me
to die? We're travelling to its last
hours to unravel my past.

Hope is a terrible thing
on a scaffold surrounded by
sounds[1] we've learned not to hear.

Tell me what they did to you.
If they're just stories, why worry?
If words can be weapons[2]

whatever happened to ours?
4.5 billion years is a long time
to remember to breathe[3]

so run like hell before you are
ejected from your time stream.
And quick-smart off my planet.

Memories can only graduate to
stories when you've relived them.
Run, get off, please?

---

[1] rebrand.ly/h1jt2o
[2] rebrand.ly/hdpx1c
[3] rebrand.ly/5yjcsy

The Husbands of River Song

Love may be even more circular than time
when it comes to husbands, which is why
the first in may also be the most lasting,

if not the best. My antlers are holographic[1]
in this silly season of detached regal heads
and my wish is for a bigger flowchart

of exoplanets saved and companions
jettisoned for their sake. King Hydroflax[2]
was River Song's third chapter, but he had this

fixation about head and diamond separation
that made romance a famine by jump cuts.
So my "Hello, Sweetie" was a kindly ace

though I never loved her back, even at Darillium's
Singing Towers, where her fictions of us
dissolved. At best it was a sunset of crystal

air where happy endings[3] are merely the lies
we tell ourselves in the dark hugs between
portals. Our slomo date of 24 years will just

have to divert.
Or do.

---

[1] rebrand.ly/75mf8a
[2] rebrand.ly/l04gsl
[3] rebrand.ly/k0rvnj

Photo: syfi.com

Series 10

Minerva: Wormholes

There's this part in *metastasis*[1]
when you throw a grenade in
and the wormhole turns orange

but then retreats back to green –
so what do you do?

*Throw in two grenades
that'll destroy it...*

Sorry, I was distracted
by chatter about some trailer
I've never played.

I really want to tell you about
black holes as time lords[2]
and the ultimate gasp

of holding on for dear death.
Here, or wherever we are when
there is here, space acts like a

fabric, watch it twist until
it can be measured, warping
space, until it loops into the past

entangling photons[3] into a future
surging faster than the speed of light.
Blue-sky thinking is the best when

we're far apart – or docking in a
fresh parallel. After all, what
we know about past and future

---

[1] rebrand.ly/k8usoo
[2] rebrand.ly/c9esv0
[3] rebrand.ly/v7522b

is up/down to math, or the debates
we play with quantum physics
anointing them as *new* thrones.

Photo: biffbampop.com

The Return of Dr Mysterio

What do I have in common with Clark Kent?[1]
Certainly not his love of skin-tight threads, but yes
keeping a phone box handy for the first threat

of danger, and being on call 24/7 to buffer
humans, especially page turning companions,
despite their impulse to hug him or me

at the drop of an alien. Save is just what we
freelancers do without bronzing or vows.
During a pause, I was trying to power up

a time distortion equaliser thingy[2] with a Hazandra
gemstone, when young boy Grant swallowed it
and developed a persistent case of levitation,

a capital G, and a blue rubber speed handy
24 years on to sidestep his part-time nanny
job for high school sweetheart Lucy

(read Lois Lane). Tagged the Ghost because
all the better comics names had been branded,
he was super as a backstop brake for a spaceship[3]

with nukes cross-haired at NYC. I *could*
have snagged it myself, but I was missing Clara
and River Song, it was Christmas again,

and everyone deserves a happy
reboot after a sad
ending.

---

[1] rebrand.ly/xxucx3
[2] rebrand.ly/l7vb6b
[3] rebrand.ly/paejyi

The Pilot

How can you doubt that poetry and physics[1]
are the same? They almost rhyme except
when they don't but even then their tune

begs to be discovered. Most people
frown when they don't understand,
but you, dear Bill, smile so of course

I'm happy to be your personal tutor[2]
about time and life – its tidepools
and cinema of memories invented

frame by frame in our specs
that can be past, present, future –
at once. You are right to puzzle

how a puddle can be right there
when it hasn't rained for weeks
and how it can reflect or even

embody the lizard you imagine
in your brain when you confront
the pilot your Heather has become.

Never mind: she only wants to kill us!
Hardly anything or one is purely evil, just
hungry, dripping with that surplus of tears[3]

and we're at the wrong end of
her cutlery portal until you release her
from her sacred promise not to go.

[1] rebrand.ly/dpy873
[2] rebrand.ly/ws3lve
[3] rebrand.ly/2h0vdc

Smile

Know what I like about humanity?
Its searing optimism, and yet with a
corkscrew in reserve – a lego place

to brick at after cryogenic dreams[1]
of a future mindful where climate
can be recoded and raw emotions

configured to tame a fussy algorithm.
Yes, Bill, I know I *promised* not to go
off-world except in emergency mode

but the Tardis has this seventh sense
that can override my steering at will
like a souped-up Tesla water-witch.

And now we're immersed in faultless
white, too early or too late to save
the waking podists,[2] especially

those scouts whose skulls have been
promised to fertiliser for the perfect
crops awaiting the mother ship.

Smile is the watchword for teams of
emoji-bots: any lesser expression
dooms you to the miscue of minerals

so, smile, Bill, *smile*, try to ignore
the horror tick-ticking down to blast,
while I try to unscramble their fatal

---

[1] rebrand.ly/wa9qm0
[2] rebrand.ly/i4kf36

code[1] for 'happiness'. How could it be as simple as pressing reset?

Photo: bbcamerica.com

―――――――――

[1] rebrand.ly/gqcj2h

Smile [distilled]

Peace for the news faked
War clouds the President's eye
Robot's smiley face.[1]

---

[1] rebrand.ly/501e7

Thin Ice

History's mortgaged by the skaters,
those who elude the monster jaws
sluicing the Thames[1] with seductive

green searchlights and who live to tell
the collateral death of those who stood
inert at the weakest link and got dragged

under for a Master menu – nothing personal,
just random. Their gurgles will fall on deaf
ears because injustice can only appeal

when reason runs off to fight another
day. Have you heard of the 'stuff' that burns
underwater hotter then coal? There's hope

for ingenuity yet, but never underestimate
that collective human ability to harness
the inexplicable.[2] Which is why I'm still

here, waiting for the snap thaw of
outrage, and the refrain of interstellar
space, which is why I never steer[3]

the Tardis, only roll with the angles
until my next episode (crisis)
blooms.

---

[1] rebrand.ly/f4zms7
[2] rebrand.ly/0a6psd
[3] rebrand.ly/x09vxm

Knock, Knock

Ah, share houses[1] – you've all
been there while you were young
and foolish, signing blind contracts

with phantom landlords – or at least
absentee ones – who mumble over
electrical flaws, and pretend to ignore

alien claws shredding the timber[2] limbs;
while outside tree spirits conspire
in leafless secrets about colonies

delayed. Meanwhile, Eliza's flesh is reconciled
to a tuning fork by pitch for her father's pride.
But what's the point in cramping a crescendo

when you have to cringe behind shutters
to preserve your frail sacks of breath?[3]
Life should be the unexpected – or not at all!

---

[1] rebrand.ly/j536bn
[2] rebrand.ly/wv3bsp
[3] rebrand.ly/ikyz0m

Knock, Knock [distilled]

Her father tune-forks space fleas[1]
to embed tenants in the woodwork
while moving van Tardis pauses

for a grandpa hotwire

Photo: tardis.fandom.com

---

[1] rebrand.ly/7vvhlz

Oxygen

Remain calm while your nervous system
is deactivated. Your unlicensed oxygen[1]
will be expelled. Our deaths are too costly

even with an excess of rescue ships.
Relax: some of my best friends
are blueish.[2]

---

[1] rebrand.ly/35pl3j
[2] rebrand.ly/xy1945

Extremis

Without Hope

our scripts unfold
to the chants of Veritas[1]
blood drops to portals

Without Witness

mysterious lights
outsmart our shining corners
book cages broken

Without Reward

the shadows test us[2]
blind in our video game
unreal synapse to pixel[3]

---

[1] rebrand.ly/pama06
[2] rebrand.ly/psgjib
[3] rebrand.ly/98zzpl

The Pyramid at the End of the World

Every trap

you walk into is
a chance to learn
where the laser points[1]

Power needs consent

so fake love is slavery[2]
hacking into sex

Watch the Doomsday Clock

tick away the pyramid
that undermines our fear

Being smart

is not
surrendering your planet[3]
for unconditional sight

---

[1] rebrand.ly/hl8ybc
[2] rebrand.ly/gfwpf6
[3] rebrand.ly/8mj94c

The Lie of the Land

Playing with history[1]
the monks tease open[2]
by proverbs, forge by statues
on every corner, shouting down

stagnation.

Pew dwellers don't second-
guess the future
of our obdurate planet –
kindness in the eye

of a virtual beholder.[3]

---

[1] rebrand.ly/4flju2
[2] rebrand.ly/05suwf
[3] rebrand.ly/1wh1j0

Empress of Mars

We are surrounded
by noisy royals[1] who think
the British Empire

is still burning bright
even under the ice of Mars.[2]
'What does the pink mass

mean?' Victorians
yearn for discovery, virginity[3]
out of reach, weaponised.

Photo: en.wikipedia.org

[1] rebrand.ly/dudoqg
[2] rebrand.ly/672nq8
[3] rebrand.ly/e4lbwv

The Eaters of Light

They will keep chewing[1]
until no planets are left
or stars to navigate by

unless we can cave
the beast into a portal
for lost Romans[2] of the Light.

Damp crows at the gateway
to sunrise as my patience
shatters; the trouble with hope[3]

is resisting its music.

[1] rebrand.ly/iobg1c
[2] rebrand.ly/xg3hk6
[3] rebrand.ly/tdzg8k

World Enough and Time

Bill, you waited for me to sonic
a cure to your mortal wound

while Missy tries to steer us free[1]
of the black hole that's squishing

your breath to a vacancy in
Mondasian space.[2] Should I have known

your upgrade was already in theatre
to a fresh Cyberman while, unmasked,

the Master asked Missy for a kiss?[3]
Genesis in two days for you means

two exoduses far too late
for our spaceship.

---

[1] rebrand.ly/wghu2s
[2] rebrand.ly/ty7azv
[3] rebrand.ly/38g8qp

The Doctor Falls

Somebody blasted our barn,
dismantling fun from cruelty.
Who was that just now, Bill,[1]

grinning while your reflection
burns, red-flagging eternal night
as my kindness[2] shudders?

Hugging still hurts my heart[3]
but pleading me back to life
will only mask my conversion's rust

and your tortured
Cyber
smile

Photo: framerated.co.uk

[1] rebrand.ly/c6g8y9
[2] rebrand.ly/hqlqua
[3] rebrand.ly/8abiy0

Twice Upon A Time

I have the game plan
to die again as a Doctor must
though something has grown

very wrong with the space
as I approach the chamber
of depleted Daleks[1]

We're no more than our
mistakes – ladies of glass,[2]
sons who mock their

fathers but a reconnected
life never hurt anyone, and
love is all the more networked

for memory on the long path
around. As my restless shadow
welcomes with feminine breath.[3]

---

[1] rebrand.ly/817b3
[2] rebrand.ly/f7su4o
[3] rebrand.ly/v9z357

Photo: bbc.co.uk

Series 11

Minerva: Second Genesis

We are ready to explore, decode
solar systems from negative dust[1]
deploy our spider-bots and drones

in our divining for maverick water,
carbon, understudy molecules.
As we biomimic[2] the voice between

silences, not distracted by ice-
whispers from Comet 67P,[3]
Rosetta arranges my samples

into sentient channels that zigzag
around black vacuums that
threaten with reckless energy.

It all boils down to puddles,
waveforms of future portals
shapeshifting before our eyes.

---

[1] rebrand.ly/2uievu
[2] rebrand.ly/oq2lfc
[3] rebrand.ly/yi6zym

Photo: uk.movies.yahoo.com

The Woman Who Fell to Earth

Once you learn how to tumble
from a bike you never forget.
Bad timing: I was in mid-transform[1]

from my grey-haired Scottish
skin (bless his sexy drawl!)
bracing for my train roof grand

entry, no time to muck about
with who I am or was or should be
though I do have this niggling

yearn for a certain runaway police-
box especially as I confront the data
coil of this flying spaghetti monster.[2]

Have I ever tasted a Hershey's Kiss?
Does it really matter as carriages uncouple
and Tzim-Sha[3] can zap us at will?

I do prefer the height-thrill of cranes
to the afterburn of virtual chocolate
as I blowtorch a fresh sonic screwdriver

from random scraps of metal. Damn
those budget cuts! We can do so much
better than purloined teeth for trophies.

Yes, always be *kind*!

---

[1] rebrand.ly/Ok0xeh
[2] rebrand.ly/lqbzgj
[3] rebrand.ly/2xy7y0

The Ghost Monument

How do we know when a planet
is in the wrong place? A triad of suns
is a dead giveaway that we still

scatter in pythagorean squares.[1]
And how do we take up sides
when 3D monuments morph

into 4D operas?[2] Forget
my slippery gender: I still have
those two hearts even if my Tardis

has gone walkabout. Holographs[3]
are easy to trick when you're dancing
for/in time, but I prefer a locked door

tempting us with a cover song of fresh
challenges. It all comes down
to familiar air and options.

Right.
Let's get our shift on.

---

[1] rebrand.ly/j8p9dr
[2] rebrand.ly/i3e2oj
[3] rebrand.ly/4rs6iz

Rosa

When people need help, I never
refuse yet how can we manoeuvre
the tipping instants of history?[1]

I lent Elvis a cell phone for
company but he was all thumbs
with that holographic guide

and couldn't see the point
of taking selfies with the cascade
of New York flashbulbs around

Meanwhile in Montgomery, Rosa Parks[2]
sits resolute so others can stand,
bannering to birth protests by people

of random colour, shouting with silence.
What a determined anthem a seamstress
can weave! Until Krasko plays the spoiler

by nudging cues from his storm cage
and tiny things ever so slightly rise up
and also stubborn numbers on a bus

in a freeze-frame of 1955 in spite
until Ryan blitzes the temporal displacement[3]
against him *living life on a merry-go-round*

while Rosa refreshes my coat just in
time to intersect her instant in history

---

[1] rebrand.ly/65jccn
[2] rebrand.ly/l96wgt
[3] rebrand.ly/1qmki9

rise up in spite of the ache a thousand

times

again

Photo: scififantasynetwork.com

Arachnids in the UK

Am I just being weird? I tried
the small talk about having a flat
and a purple couch but I slipped

into stage fright mode[1] when I told them
about the aqua hospital and being
a Sister to a camp for assassins.

I do love a conspiracy but not a month's
worth of spider tram lines strewn in a day
from carcasses breeding in a toxic dump

underpinning ultra-Jack Robertson's luxury
hotel, not so inert just to exhale
methane but certainly wakeful enough

to inhale growth hormones and cocoon
typecast humans for a rainy day. 21 quadrillion
and counting but who's counting when they

can burst through bathtubs and subscript
bodyguards? "Run now, ask questions
later!" shouts Graham, and that's top advice.

Let's put a door between us and that ad
break for Imperfect Vertical Integration.[2]
And why isn't Ed Sheeran running in 2020

with lines like Darling just dive right in
And follow my lead yes, yes, Yes!
But while Ryan pipers the spider babes

---

[1] rebrand.ly/93suwn
[2] rebrand.ly/jyl5Oo

into some Panic Room with his hashtag
vibration rap[1] (the best novel I never wrote)
hey where do you know me from?

Jack guns down their mum in the ballroom
in the name of "civilisation" post-Trump.
Sad. More than sad. But now we're Fam,

Team Tardis. Yeah, I dig it, man, yeah.

---

[1] rebrand.ly/8b7f0

The Tsuranga Conundrum

The problem with junk galaxies is
their planets all look the same when
you trip over a sonic mine and then

get teleported into a remote controlled
hospital future sans exits but vibrations
in excess! Something's penetrated

our shields: a muncher of non-organics,[1]
Pting is pint-sized, almost cuddly, until
it snatches, chews and spits out my sonic

like granola, leaving it limp and smoking
to my disbelief. The toxic nerve of it!
Chief Medical Officer, Astos, is a bit

of a dish, but he gets jettisoned before
my second heart can even skip a beat
while some bloke is going into labour

without a birth-bud[2] after just three weeks'
gestation (his luck for not taking precautions!)
which is enough to spark my sonic back to life

and me to reflect on the joys of anti-
matter and how to lure Pting[3] to a dessert
of antimony – the ultimate energy gulp!

It all comes down to candy floss, Lego,
problem to be solved but mostly hope
as we pivot on worlds of imagination

ducking through asteroid showers

[1] rebrand.ly/fpwopj
[2] rebrand.ly/fh6w8t
[3] rebrand.ly/9swmnx

Demons of the Punjab

This is what unravels when
you're too nice and the wrong word
at the wrong moment interferes

you out of existence: barefooted served
the Wise Man[1] well until a bullet
from 17 August 1947 sectioned

his body from his spirit while impossible
creatures chanted over forgotten
corpses. Demons from the Thejarian[2]

surprise us with their auras and we
cannot disrupt their work in the yowling
cracks of this reconfigured landscape

as they, no longer assassins, do bear
witness to the thick harmonies of time
and the healing power of love that

protects the future against the hatred
closing in from all sides when even
ordinary people lose their minds.

Whew!

And so Umbreen and Prem,[3]
stand-ins for Juliet and Romeo,
tease and untangle our DNA.

---

[1] rebrand.ly/771d20
[2] rebrand.ly/vknn2h
[3] rebrand.ly/7znicw

Kerblam!

My Turkish hat surprise –
is it still me? Or some
encrypted HELP ME sob

slipping through the trip
wires of a macro marketeer?[1]
Still can't get into the swing

behind going organic and
though some of my best
enemies are robots I'm tempted

to bedevil these conveyor belts.[2]
Who can chill out when those
Group Loop eyes monitor

our every move? Kerblam
is such a well-oiled op
with a tailored box to suit

any wish – but loving my hat!
like Charlie and Kira, his 9 to 5
crush, so innocent smelling so

perfect – until she gets
confused down in the Triple 9s
mistaking that respect must run

both ways. *HELP ME* yet again
as we poke sticks in a wasp's
hive of conspiracy,[3] detected

---

[1] rebrand.ly/kex1y5
[2] rebrand.ly/z5xiud
[3] rebrand.ly/qebjdf

by Dispatch as organic
contaminates and rogue lip
reading. But isn't Twirlie

so hot? With synapses too
crowded to detect liquified
bombs in the bubblewrap.

The System's on auto-pilot
for naughty parcels counting
down to the final KERBLAM!

Teach you to play
with a stranger's bubblewrap,
Charlie!

Photo: imbd.com

The Witchfinders

When you're the apple in a bob
for witches you can't win:
either way you're horse meat

sinew for Satan by the barbs
of Mistress Becka Savage[1] –
(set a woman to hang a woman

for our aptitude for gossip
and our flattened team structure).
And King Jim loves a fleck of flirtation[2]

on the side, with gender no object,
such a cross dressing of the mind,
with his stash of body parts to purify

any sprout of mud tendrils whispering
Insurrection. Small wonder he trusts
no one, bat-caving behind his mask

of velvet words that he prances out
like a hero: *evil be to him that evil
thinks* even as the darkness snarls

back at him. But there's a hint of poetry
oozing from the pauses, a Morax
of alien revenge[3] who will not kill

but fill you with limbo matter to
wonder at those wands of the heart
we dismiss as dark magic.

[1] rebrand.ly/1csdip
[2] rebrand.ly/b66y27
[3] rebrand.ly/kcr7ly

It Takes You Away

A Norwegian cottage with no chimney
in winter is like a blind girl deserted
by her dad for a love-nest

in some frilly dimension. Solitract[1]
can pierce through a layer of three
locks to plunk down eight dead birds side

by side. It takes you away
through the jittering mirror
to a portal where reflections

are an after-taste (tragedy always
makes me hungry) to the Anti-zoned
Ribbons of the Seven Stomachs[2]

(now I've *lost* my appetite) who
has a sweet tooth for tubulars
(mine) and smells of wee –

(not his) more spoils for flesh-eating
moths. All this for a detoured dad?
It's a sleight of sonic in this reverse

Plane where Trine pretends
to keep house and Grace tempts
Graham[3] to dream in holographs

as reality collapses, and furniture
gains a pulse. But a shapeshifting
frog as the Solitract? What's this

[1] rebrand.ly/5e35a
[2] rebrand.ly/yvw4s7
[3] rebrand.ly/ixnfc0

multiverse coming to? It's maddest,
even beautiful, and out there
breathing might just be a Gallifreyan

god.

Photo: blogtorwho.com

Battle of Ranskoor AV

Dis-integrator of us all: how's that
for a planet not to be missed?
Just when I thought we'd learned

how little we actually can know,
the Tardis logs in no less than nine,
yes, nine urgent texts, so naturally

we have to trace them to source
where the fuss is all about unfinished
business and a dazed commander

who made the mistake of venturing
outdoors without a neurobalancer[1]
to calm his mind − and trigger

finger. It's 3407 years since their
'Creator' arrived, and the Ux[2]
are quite disarmed by his armour

and the fake truths he bristles
to keep them and those capsuled nine
planets in limbo, but I can disrobe

a demigod when I scan him
and those last seven years must
have really been a drag for T'zim-

Sha, hobbled by a stasis
of his own sketching, deadly
tentacles with consequences

---

[1] rebrand.ly/cz12x9
[2] rebrand.ly/sun7bl

for a High Noon with Graham
intent on revenging his Grace[1]
once their telepathic circuits

collide. And so the Universe
has a surprise in store: a shot
in the foot the final insult

sealing him hermetically in his
pride. Which reminds me:
have I mentioned that I half-

invented the Wellington?

Photo: pajiba.com

---

[1] rebrand.ly/k25j07

Resolution

Amazing what you find unburied in thirds
or what can be riveted with junkyard chic[1]
and cosmic memory when you're a Dalek

Scout itchy within a squid's skin.
And yes it's *personal* between us
sort of a sonic blind date[2]

to settle a feud much longer
than a shrinking Milky Way.
And I wouldn't be so panicky

if I knew where we were headed –
then again what rescues would be
skipped if the Tardis just throttles

dust? So once more into the breach
dear Fam: New Year's a precious time[3]
to save the Earth, and forgive your dad!

Photo: digitalspy.com

[1] rebrand.ly/1ltomh
[2] rebrand.ly/jxxmq8
[3] rebrand.ly/lw6aay

Series 12 (a taster)

Minerva: Pyrocene

My sensors have picked up surface flares
from the crust of a promising exoplanet
a mere 18796 light years away from our probe.

We have discounted the instigation of meteor
strikes but cannot rule out dry gasp thunder or
premeditation[1] by connatural or alien species.

If life resists there beyond the conflagration,
I trust that it will learn from the delicate
regeneration that Nature insists upon beyond

the eonic arrogance
of "intelligent"
beings.

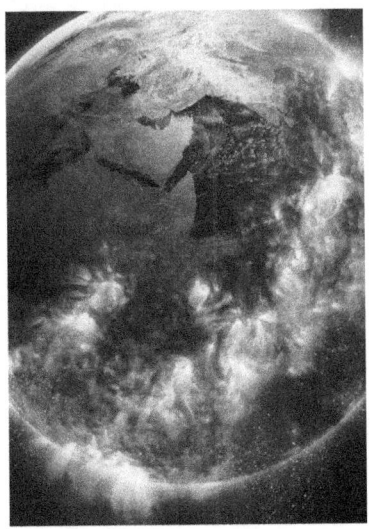

Image: wallpapersmug.com

---

[1] rebrand.ly/mijalb

Photo: digitalspy.com

Spyfall 1

When it comes to spies, trust no one.
Especially that slick Daniel Barton, a
triple agent,[1] an ego only 93% human

and a tux to rival James Bond to boot.
The innocents have taken their eyes off
the horizon and defaulted their critical

mass to Siri, Alexa, while MI6 agents
everywhere suffer the same laser shock.
We're targeted by shades of alien glare[2]

who can bypass our invisible shields,
teleporting Yasmin – and even me! –
to a netherworld of charcoaled trees,

while corporate VOR absorbs your data,
wiping then reformatting human DNA
for its doomsday scenario.[3] When we

stowaway on Barton's private jet
the spy-MASTER plays his trump:
a cockpit bomb that I can't –

SNAP!!

---

[1] rebrand.ly/443a4
[2] rebrand.ly/bd901
[3] rebrand.ly/s0m6qow

Spyfall 2

I'm talking to myself, so I must still
be alive! OK, so the Master is also
the spy Master, and he gets a thrill

in both hearts when he kills with
his Incredible Shrinking Device for
the love of chaos. But I can do classic

too, recoding Kasavins[1] across multiple
dimensions, as we nip and tuck from
steamy 1834 to Nazi 1943, time fugitives

from Gallifrey (we have that in common)
but not his arson, conflating our planet
into a lie of fiery monoliths. All future

lost? No, Fam, where there's risk there's
hope, but consumers kept clicking 'Agree'[2]
to Barton's fine-print proof of concept

so he could reformat, convert every device
at once, declaiming that humanity is done:
"Welcome to the end of your life!"

But I'm still a big fan of staying alive
and playing guardian to heartbeats above
the floorboards,[3] so I knell for the Master

---

[1] rebrand.ly/nszsdi0
[2] rebrand.ly/41sh868
[3] rebrand.ly/6dqd4ws

(fingers crossed behind my back) –
after planting a virus in the VOR server
and cuing in the Gestapo to arrest him

as double-spy. You see, Darkness never
sustains, though it lingers on long enough
to expose the true skin of a timeless child.

Photo: blogterwho.com

Orphan 55

If it's free, it's too good to be true:
Tranquility Spa and Refreshment Zone.
How much of that voucher was false?

There's a spa, true, but steaming with
Dregs (more on them later), and the Zone
chucks out bags of chips with a hopper virus[1]

worm that sent Ryan truly dancing. So
tranquility's a relative state, depending on
what spirits you're slurping on your lounge

by the purified pool. "Blimey!" shouts Graham,
flattening his nose on my fresh iconic membrane
that seals off the hype from the host landscape

of Orphan 55, making Gallifrey look like
some Disney-world with its angry trees[2] and
oxygen countdown. At 2%, I need to talk less

and sonic more! Yes, the Dregs were marooned
once the humans abandoned Earth after the
Doomsday Clock clanged true, and they aren't

game for a good 'ol passive aggressive chat
about how their future might have been patched
if the pollies had argued less about the washing up

and noticed your house was burning down.[3] Now,
this dream-bubble of 'tranquility' is all that lingers
with its deflating oxygen and inexorable Dregs,

---

[1] rebrand.ly/cgbkelh
[2] rebrand.ly/953e0
[3] rebrand.ly/8fe6e

sucking CO_2.

Photo: blogs.weta.org

Nikola Tesla's Night of Terror

No, this is not a tale of autonomous cars, but scorpion
invaders from Mars. I suppose Nikola had it coming
pinning his ear to the night waves. Then when he heard

a chatter of sorts, he had the brash to prattle back. He
should have known something was up from that pesky
Thassa Orb[1] spying on him mid-air with a greenish AC

but he was too busy inventing the 20th century before
that pretender Edison could cash in on his DC. It
wasn't just that Nikola reminded me of David Bowie

in that gilded New York City[2]: he also created alone,
in parentheses to the money-grabbers, too impatient
to let the world inch at a tortoise pace. But I digress:

The Queen of the Skithra wants to nab him before
he's recognised for being good at the impossible
(like me again!) Either he agrees to engineer her ship

or she'll Galli-fry Earth – a time-sensitive offer. He's
tempted. At least she's acknowledged his brilliance
and his sacrifice could be a legacy. Not on my watch!

Issuing Queenie with an airspace eviction notice
I give her one last chance to evolve. She refuses.
What else can you expect from a parasite with a kink

---

[1] rebrand.ly/bopvpg8
[2] rebrand.ly/lazqlsp

in her neck? Bring it on! While Yasmin decoys her Skithra hordes through the back alleys, we charge Nikola's Wardenclyffe Tower[1] with a bolt that zaps

the mother ship quicker than 5G – all in a day's doctoring! Poor Nikola dies penniless, but like I say you have to save Earth before you can change it.

Photo: denofgeek.com

---

[1] rebrand.ly/11v2r6g

Where it all began...

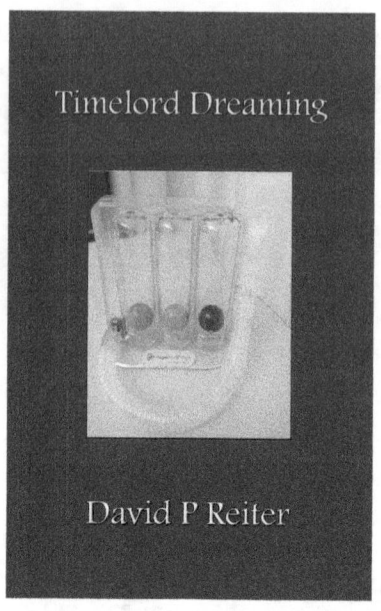

This intriguing electronic book is written in short sections the author describes as 'tweetems', which give a sense of the sometimes confusing world experienced by a patient in hospital. Acting as memory snippets, the fragments build a story; each short narrative segment being enhanced by links to web-based content that enlarges on the 'tweetem' text. The reader is taken on a surreal journey, and can choose when to follow links for more information and when to move on to the next piece of the narrative.

– Judges' report, 2016 Western Australian Premier's Award

.

www.ingramcontent.com/pod-product-compliance
Lightning Source LLC
Chambersburg PA
CBHW070043030726
47506CB00003B/837